This is something about self-forgiveness.

OTHER BOOKS BY ROBERT M. DRAKE

Spaceship (2012)

Science (2013)

Beautiful Chaos (2014)

Black Butterfly (2015)

A Brilliant Madness (2015)

Beautiful and Damned (2016)

Broken Flowers (2016)

Seed Of Chaos (2017)

Gravity: A Novel (2017)

Moon Theory (2017)

Young & Rebellious (2018)

Chasing The Gloom (2018)

Samuel White & The Frog King (2018)

For Excerpts and Updates please follow:

Instagram.com/rmdrk
Facebook.com/rmdrk
Twitter.com/rmdrk

ISBN: 978-0-9986293-5-3

Book Cover: Robert M. Drake
Cover Image licensed by Shutter Stock Inc.

For Sevyn,

All my words are yours.
All of my words, will always be yours.

CONTENTS

CHAOS THEORY

ROBERT M. DRAKE

OTHER TIMES

As long as you're here,
I never worry about
tomorrow,

for today

I am falling
and tomorrow

I am flying.

And sometimes
the difference between the two
matters,

while other times

it doesn't.

NAKED EYES

Sometimes
people get lost
the moment you try
to find them.

The same way
you never receive love
the moment
you begin looking for it.

Those are the things
we learn as we live,

people come
and go

as they please

and sometimes

love appears
to disappear

right before

your naked eyes.

WITH YOU

Tell me why
you're always so quiet.

I need to know
what you've been through.

Tell me how
you never found your smile
and why you're infatuated
with brokenness.

Tell me how
you've traveled far
into the deepest parts
of *yourself*

and how you came out
empty handed.

Tell me why
you're still hurting
when you've lost your heart
many years ago.

Tell me how
the love of your life
never returned to you
and tell me why

you haven't been able
to move on.

Tell me all the things
I need to hear
to sympathize with you…

to feel something with you…

to remind us
why we are here
together
but ultimately
still alone.

Tell me why
you're empty
and why you've been chasing
wild moons
without a proper satellite.

Tell me about your past
and why your bones
have never healed.

Tell me about your art
and how it's carefully crafted
with loneliness.

Tell me why
you apologize

for being yourself
and why
you, at times,
feel like someone else.

Tell me about your stolen laughter
and what you're hiding
beneath that sad smile.

Take your time
and tell me all these things
about you.

I want to know
because you're different

and I'm attracted
to the way you rob me
of my air.

So please,
let it out,

let out the chaos
under your ribcage.

Do it now
without thinking about it twice
and do it now

because everyone needs to believe…

that somewhere,
deep down inside,

someone down the line
really does care.

Do it now
for courage
and do it now

for all the things
that make you who you are.

Do it now
for yourself
and do it now

for me.

I am with you,
forever

and the gods
are always looking
out for the way
you feel.

FIRST TIME

Somewhere,
someone
is noticing how beautiful
people can be.

So do good,
be good.

And stay good
to others plus yourself.

You never know
whose life you're changing

for the very
first time.

TEARS AND HOME

This is why
it hurts
the way it hurts.

Because sometimes life feels
like a sequence of photos
and they're all flashing
in the blink of an eye.

Because before you know it—
the moment is gone.

Because every time someone says
I love you—a miracle happens.

Because life is madness
and your heart is chaos

and some way they both
sometimes get along.

Because watching the one
you love leave
feels like you're dying.

Because sometimes
change is the hardest thing
in the world

and because

sometimes tears
can remind you

of home.

ONE PERSON

The way you love
and the way

you're loved

are two
very strange things.

Both are never the same

and sometimes
one person

gives more
than the other

could ever give

if their lives depended
on it.

NO MATTER

No matter how far you go.
No matter how hard it gets.
No matter who you meet
and who you let go.

Always remember one thing.
Always remember to know
where you are,
who you are
and why you are
the way you are.

Always remember
that everything you encounter,
every mistake, every flaw
and every moment
is bringing you closer
toward the edge of your life.

Toward the doom
we can't run away from.

So know where you stand,
know yourself
and learn so much of it

that when you fade
into the stars…

you could look back
and say to yourself:

*"I tried,
I loved and I learned
to let go."*

And the universe
will respond
and say:

*"Welcome back.
I've missed you
and worry not,*

*I know you did all
that you could."*

MY BOOKS

I sell my sadness
on paper

as if
it were gold

and maybe it is

because as people read it,

they change, they heal.

My sadness
takes broken people,
sad people
and gives them
the hopethey need

to love again.

What a beautiful way to live.

To inspire those around you
out of what deeply hurts.

I am truly blessed
and so…
are you.

SLIPPING AWAY

You have lived this
sheltered live.

Like a small child
looking out the window
as it rains.

And

that's not necessarily
a terrible thing.
It is just you haven't experienced
the world for what it is,

for what it makes you feel.

I mean, sure,
there are terrible things happening.

Famine, genocide,
kidnappings and slavery.

The list goes on.

And because of these devilish things,
these things
that kill the spirit,
you fear life itself.

You don't live on the edge.

Now by that,
I don't mean having to
drink with sharks.

By that, I mean,
you have got to take a chance
on yourself,
on your potential.

You have got to believe
in yourself
and know
how you have so much to see,
to lose.

And time, well,
that's another tricky little bastard
that keeps slipping away.

Little by little, therefore,
you have to use it wisely.

You only have one life
and the clock is ticking.

Let the seconds that ring
remind you
of how much breath
you have left in you

to use.

The world is still
a beautiful place

and only you
could fall in love

with it

in such a way
that only you

could describe how.

DAY WE MET

I think what hurts
the most is,

how we never got
a second chance.

How my hands
miss the way yours feel.

And how

we'll live our lives
believing
that what we once had

was doomed
from the very first day
we met.

MAYBE, WHO KNOWS...

Maybe she was your favorite person
but you only wanted her around
when you felt alone.

She wasn't meant
to fix you.
She wasn't meant
to wait around for you
to reach her.

She was meant to be more.

For she is the air
that gives you breath
and you have been living
your life... underwater.

Appreciate her
before you drown.

Love her now
before someone else
does.

NEVER LIES

No one knows
what they want.

Life is sort of
this long journey
of trying to figure
things out

but in the end,

no one knows
what's going on.

But that's a secret
and trust me
when I say
all of them

are never lies.

RAWNESS AND SADNESS

There is more to her
than just flesh and bone,
rawness and sadness,

love and confusion.

There is more to her
than what meets the eye.

Believe me
when I tell you,
when you finally understand her,

you will know,

how some women
have more within them
than others

and how some of them
should never be tamed.

So let her go.

Let her spread her wings
and she will always find you
in the wild.
Where the moon

and the sun,

all skies
and all oceans collide…

at the very
same time.

LOVE THEM

You don't
lose yourself
as time goes on,

or as you meet
more people.

You find yourself
in them.

People complete
other people.

Sometimes,
they make them feel
better
about loving
themselves.

CLEAN BLOOD

Let go of the riot
in your heart.

Let it out
because the violence
on your hands
makes your arms heavy

and you need them
to heal
the broken people
around you.

Clean the blood
from your hands
and you will see
how they possess more
than fingers,

more
than a clenched fist
full of lost hope,
broken dreams
and sad forgiveness.

Let go of the pain
you're holding,
free your hands,

rid them of the suffering
your laws have created.

Let go of your weapons.
Let go of your sins.

Free your hands
of all things
that trouble the fire.

Free them
and they will create miracles.

They will build churches,
schools and shelters.

Your hands will touch faces,
wipe tears and carry smiles.

Let go of the riot
in your heart.

Let go of the regret.

Today is a new day
to hold on to the differences
that make us who we are.

Today is a new day
to feel the days,
the nights and inbetween.

Today we should all
hold hands

and never…

ever…

let go.

THIS TIME

After all this time,
I should have known
you'd be the end of me.

I should have known
distance was not a cure
but the disease
that tore us further apart.

And it broke me.
It left me empty inside
and what's worse is

how I'd probably
let it happen all over again.

You see,
we almost made it, kid,

we almost did
and it could have been
beautiful
but now

it's too late.

YEARS AND YEARS

It took me years
to understand
that some people
do not change,
cannot change.

And no matter how many chances
you have given them,
it always goes the same way.

And it never ends.

They go,
while you arrive,
and believe me,
it's hard to arrive.

It's hard to pluck yourself
for other people.

To break apart for them.
To meet side by side
and understand them
for who they are.

It's hard when people don't
see things as you do.

You change,
you grow
and you love yourself.

And the more you do,
the less the bullshit
people bring

upsets you.

FROM WITHIN

People can't destroy you,
break you or hurt you.

Only you
have the power to do

that

to yourself.

The chaos always
comes
from within.

IF I GO

If I go,
that is,
if I choose to accept
the harsh reality
of loneliness.

Just know
that whoever fills my place
once I'm gone,
will, too,
eventually
wander off.

Whether it be,
physically or mentally.

Here or there.
Up or down.
Far or near.

Whoever comes next
will arrive
when you need them most
and abort
when they must,

that is,

when you least expect it.

Understand
that life goes on.

The rain will pour
and the sun will flare.

Understand
that nothing is meant
to be yours.

That lovers are not meant
to be forever...

that you are born alone
and cold,
and numb of feelings
and loss of words,

they will go.

I will go
and at times,
you, too, will go,

although,

you don't like
the idea of leaving.

We are all meant
to go through life alone.

We are all meant
to go through
a parade of people.

We are all meant
to take what we can
because it is all we know.

We are all meant to grasp,
whether we cry or laugh.

Alone.
Always alone.

Just you
and the long road ahead.

Understand this,
and you will have the world
in the palm of your hand.

You will kiss the gods
and they…

will kiss you back.

WE SEEK YOU

And one day
we will become
what we seek:

the love we have grown
to know
but have never
been able to feel…

*the days we have lost
and the memories
we can never have back.*

One day
you will be mine
and I will be everything
you need

as long

as it means
something to you.

THE POWERS BE

The people
keep giving power
to the powers
that divide them.

The people
continue to feed
the beast
that influences the children.

They let loose
the fires that burn
the future.

There is no hope.
There is no freedom.
There is no choice,
not even within yourself.

But that's what they want.

As long as you give them
everything you own,
they won't kill you.

And they will *take it*
one way or another.

Whether it is
inyour education.
In your house.
In your car.
Your family.

They will take it all.

And if they don't,
they will leave you in debt.
One you cannot outrun.

Debt is the devil.
It is worse than jail.

Shit!

As if the stresses of live
aren't bad enough.

With them running the world,
what chances do the
children have?

The banks
and the corporations
want it all.

Even our children
and then
they want change

for the children.

Yes, of course they do
but as long
as it doesn't interrupt
the flow of their money,
of your money
into their fat pockets.

How else do they expect
the change they preach?

The false hope
they advertise in the commercials.

They give you a house,
a car, a life,
as long as it is on their terms.

And god forbid
you don't agree with them,
because then
you're an enemy
that is,
if you don't adapt.

Then you're crazy.

A loose cannon
waiting to crash
into the middle of the sea.

Please take all of me,
but for Christ's sake,
do not take my daughters,
our sons.

The children are not free.
The children are not safe.
The children are trapped.

Please take all of me,
but for Christ's sake,
save the children, *free them.*

Tell them where the love is.

Show them where hope dwells,
teach them to be better.

Teach them to put their dreams
in themselves and in people.

Not in cars,
houses, jewelry, etc.

Make them feel,
make them believe
that there is more to life
than working
to pay your bills,

to fill their banks

with their money.

Let them learn.
Let them adapt.

And above all,

let them change the ways
of the old world.

So they can respark
the love that has gone
missing.

MOST VALUE

It's hard when your lover
turns into a stranger

and it's even harder
when you close your eyes
and they're still there.

Memories kill,
and sometimes
the most valuable lesson
a lover could ever
teach you is

the importance of forgiveness
and letting

it all

just go.

NOT EASY

Life's hard.
It's not supposed to be easy.

I mean,
do you have any idea
how hard your heart pumps
just to keep you alive?

Or how hard your body works
just to keep everything
in you intact?

No, of course not,
because you ignore the signs,
the feelings
and live your life thinking
that's okay,

that you'll eventually
get another chance.

But life doesn't work that way.

You've got to listen to yourself,
trust and do things
for yourself.

And like your body,

you should be fighting
for the things that give you life,
the things you love,

and not because you want to
but because
you need to.

Everything starts
the moment you begin
and paradise will always
reveal itself to those

who fight
the good fight
a little harder.

Remember that.

I NEED YOU

What I have with you,
I don't want with someone else

and deep down in inside
I know
what we have is special.

And I know
because I'm trying to live
with you and without you.

I'm trying to want you
and let you go.

I'm trying to convince myself
you're no good for me

but I need you...

at the same time.

What a terrible dilemma
to have…

To keep and let go
at the very

same time.

WYNWOOD AGAIN

I was in Wynwood,
doing the usual
when I decided to grab a drink
at the wood tavern.

I had two gooses before
I had it in me
to talk to anyone.

The bartender was swaying
and the music was loud enough
to silence my thoughts.

Soon enough,
a girl comes next to me.
She orders a beer
and we begin talking.

We do the usual.

Where are you from?
Where do you work?

Type of conversation.

We talked for a long time
and then
she began to talk

about her favorite TV shows.

She spoke of Breaking Bad,
Sex in the City,
Dare Devil and a few others.

Then I went ahead
and asked her
about the Walking Dead.

She said
she had never heard of it.

Now come on, she had never heard
of my favorite show?

That was blasphemous!

That was the last time
I spoke to her
and I never regretted it.

I hope I never run
into her again.

PETALS ON GROUND

Sometimes
I break
in all the softest
of places...

and sometimes

I feel like
the petals
on the ground.

TO THE HOLY ONE

I need you
to protect me
from all the things
that devour me.

From all things
that damage the soul
but break it in a way
that feels good.

From all things
past, present, and both:
sad and happy.

From all the things
that break nations apart.

All things that must happen…
like wars, tears,
and the fear
that fills the hearts of brave men.

Protect me, old,
holy, beautiful one.

Show me the way
to across the universe.

Show me how
to brace myself
when the darkness comes.

Show me where the sun is.
Show me where the path
to perfect righteousness is.

Show me
because I am coming
and protect me
because I am hopeful.

I need you
to save me

from all the things
I think I love.

A DAMN THING

Maybe somewhere,
in another world,
in another dimension,

you and I are together,

sharing a moment,

a drink

and not thinking
of a damn thing.

A PERSON IS...

I don't know
what I want

and what's funny is,
how everyone
might seem as if they have it
all figured out,

but in all truth,
they don't.

And like you,
someone, too,
might see you
and think:

*"There goes a person
who has their life
together,
who knows exactly
where they're going,"*

But in all aspects,
it's madness.

Everyone thinks they know
what they want
but the problem is,

they don't know
how to get it
for themselves.

And when they get it
they don't want it
or know
what to do with it.

What you desire is an illusion
and *nothing is real*

until

it is gone.

SOME WOMEN I KNOW

And now
they have almost
all the women believing
they are not enough,

because they want
the women
to believe that their minds
and hearts
are not beautiful.

That only their bodies
can be appreciated
and loved.

But I tell
my fellow strong women
this:

You are more
than just a pretty face.

Your mind is gold
and your heart is where
the diamonds lie.

It is just,
most people

do not want to put in
enough effort to find
what truly
makes you beautiful.

And to be honest,
this is another thing
they don't tell you:

You are a goddamn
work of art
and you do not need
some asshole art dealer
to tell you

your worth

because I know your value.

You are priceless, baby,
and I just want you

to see that
for yourself.

That is all.

OCEANS BOTTOM

And I know
how broken you are,
how heavy you feel,

but still,

you have to find
the light in you.

You have to
hold on to it
with care
and never let go,

even if it drags you
toward bottom
of the ocean.

THE

The music business.
The film business.
The book business.

It's all the same.

The lover.
The soul taker.
The devourer of worlds.

They're all the same.

The car dealer.
The bank loan.
The education system.

It's all the same.

The liar.
The thief.
The murderer.

They're all the same.

They arrive with a smile.
They tell you
they want to be friends.
They convince you

they want to help you,
to rob you oftalent,
of your sweat
and tears.

It may seem
toogood to be true,

but

all businesses
want to fuck youover.

It's just
some do it
harder than others...

while others do it
soft enough
for you to not even notice

what's really
going on.

STARTING OVER

It's a beautiful thing,
looking back
at your memories.

You go away
for a brief moment,
see your mistakes,

laugh at the way
it happened and then,

you realize
that you want
what most people want,

the ability to pick yourself up
and start over,

every time
you fall.

I DO NOT UNDERSTAND

I understand now,
how both men and women
are ultimately the same.

They both forgive
at the cost of losing someone,
even if they know
they weren't at fault.

They both feel
when hurt,
feel
when beaten
and feel
when the feet
on their bodies ache,

from chasing
all the wrong people.

They both yearn for love,
for attention
and for a chance to be held
those last few seconds
before they fall asleep.

The similarities are endless,
this I tell you…

but out of all things
you could name…

there is one particular thing
they have greatly in common…

and it is
how both men and women,

regardless of race,
culture, environment,
intelligence, etc.

They all breakdown
the moment they realize
how hard it is to move on.

How hard it is to walk away.

The fight is real
when the people they need the most
aren't willing to stay.

That life
and sometimes, hope

is the most powerful thing
in the world.

A LONG MILE

That's the thing about me.
I still wonder about you, sometimes

and I don't know
what's worse,
the fact that you gave me
so much
or the fact that you took it
all away.

But that's how it all
goes down, right?

When you know,
you just know, right?

Like when I knew
I fell in love with you

and when I knew
you fell out of it
with me.

They both happened quickly
and I saw them both coming
from a mile away.

Those are the types of things

you can never out run.

They just come out
suddenly,

and when they do,
they devour

you whole.

STORM ONE

Love me now
before I break
in all soft places,

before I crash
in the letters
that spell out your name

and I lose myself
in my very own
storm.

PEOPLE DIE

People die
and it doesn't necessarily mean
they're buried in the ground.

Sometimes
people die
when things change
and when they do
so suddenly.

Like when you're replaced,
forgotten or ignored.

And no one wants to be
any of those.

No one really wants to die.
No one really wants to be buried
in the ground.

People want to live
in other people's hearts,
and it's sad to say,

that most hearts
are mad,
wild rivers either
full of or starved of love…

and none of us
know what we want
and most of us

don't even know why
we feel
the things we feel.

AND AND AND

And yes,
there are
a million things
to do.

A million things
to say.

And a million things
to feel.

But none of them
are as important
as right now,

and right now,

I'm going to say
what I'm going to do
because I feel it
in me.

I need you to know
that I'll cross my heart
and hope to die

if only

it provesto you,

that somewhere
in the heart
of humanity

a rich goodness still
subsides.

IN RETURN

It's okay to lose yourself
in people.

It's okay to trust them,
help them,
and save them
to watch them grow.

It's okay to cry,
to break apart,
and feel a little more
than you should.

It's okay to be vulnerable.
It's okay to care,
and fight for what is yours.

It's okay to do
such things
and not know why.

Some people are like that.
Some people love
more than others
and never ask

for anything in return.

WE LET GO

I don't know why
it is
that some of us
are infatuated
with the idea of letting go,

but maybe
it's because
all our lives
we're born to believe
that this is the only way
we can express
the freedom we deserve.

We let go of people
to prove
how much we love them.

We let go of reality
to chase our dreams.

We let go of the truth,
if only the lies bring comfort
to our pain.

We let go of the rules
for growth,
for change

and we let go of ourselves
when what we carry within
is too damn heavy
to bear.

We let go, we let in,
and like this
we survive.

We evolve.

We let go
when we hurt,
and we let go
when we love.

And sometimes
letting go makes us better people

and sometimes
it happens several different times,

but too often,

it ends up
feeling the same.

BETWEEN THIS

I get it,
almost everything in this life
happens either too late
or too soon.

Too fast or too slow.

You end up
where you belong,
not where you think
you belong

and there's a big difference
between that.

DIE OR LIVE

I have to know
that every moment

I can either choose
to die or live.

And right now,
I'm ready
for a new hour.

A new day.
A new year.

And I am coming
like a hurricane

in a world filled
with sea.

FOR FRIENDS, ALWAYS

I want to let you know
that the world isn't
as terrible as it seems.

That the people
who make it hard,

once loved
and were once
loved in return.

I want to let you know
that if there is any chance
of finding peace,

then it begins
with you
and those around you.

I want to let you know
that everyday
can be something
worth living for,

that is,

if you let it be.
The world

and its people
are still beautiful

and only love
and friendship

can save us all.

KNOW IT OR NOT

Sometimes one person
can save you
from another person

and you don't even know
that you're being saved.

Sometimes
that is what it takes
to move on.

Like when someone goes away
they leave you empty

but soon enough
someone else fills that space.

The same way
people learn to adapt

but have no idea
they are adapting,

growing, and continuing.

Life doesn't end
when someone walks away...

it keeps going,

you keep accepting
and searching

whether you know it
or not.

ISOLATION IS GIFT

Some people
don't like
to be alone.

Some people
have no patience
that they fall
in love quicker
than they fall
out of it.

They live fast
and expose themselves
even faster.

They forget why
they are in search
of love
to begin with.

Some even try
to revive old flames,
to not feel the burn
of solitude.

Some do anything,
even risk their own lives
for a little company.

It almost becomes
a sickness...

this fear of abandonment,
of the unknown.

This fear of complete isolation.

some but not all,
have this terrible misunderstanding
of what is needed
to survive
and believe me,

solitude is bliss
and sometimes being alone
is the greatest gift
this world
has to offer.

YOUR TEARS

Save your tears
for the good things
in life.

Fight hatred with love.
Destruction with growth.

The unknown with discovery.
And sadness with laughter.

Do all good things
with true passion

and never give up

for we all have several
good fights in us.

Remember,
if it rains,
you must keep the show going
no matter what

and no matter who
shows up

at all cost.

BECAUSE OF THIS

She tells me how things are.

She defines war,
peace and even love.

She dictates it
so delicately
that I almost fall
at the mercy of her words.

She seems to know it all,
or at least enough
to have me
where she wants me.

Now,
on the edge of her palm,
she breaks me,
saves me
and like all broken things
she tries to collect me
to fix me.

And she does,
she always finds a way
to calm the storms
I harbor within.

She heals me.

She makes me feel
as if I am true...

as if I *exist.*

And maybe I do
or maybe I don't

but it is all
so fucking lovely
and in a strange way…
she makes me feel
as if I am in love.

And because of that
I am grateful to her.

She is my moon
and I am just another

person

completely in love
with the way

she lights up
my dark sky.

NO WORDS

I don't have
the perfect words.

I never have.

So don't expect me
to beg
or cry
or do whatever it is
I'm meant to do,

that is,

to make you stay.

If you want to slip away
from my life,
so be it.

If you want to
wander off,
then go ahead
be my guest.

I don't need special words
to send you to hell
because I've had enough people
walk out on me

and to be honest,

I'm okay with that.

I trust myself more
than anybody else.

PPL YOU LOVE

The people you love
are always reaching out

and yet,
some days,

you think you are alone.

You think no one gets it,
that no one understands you

but they do.

Everyone gets it.

Everyone is going through
the same struggle.

Some worse than others
but ultimately,
the same.

So please,
don't ignore those
who love you,

pay attention to them,
grow and walk with them

and believe
how miracles tend to happen

when nothing
else can.

BEAUTIFUL THING

Sometimes

a second with you
feels like a lifetime

and sometimes

breaking apart in your arms
feels like

the most beautiful thing
in the world.

AT LEAST ONE

And yes,
maybe I have gone
a little mad.

Maybe I do spend
most of my time
wondering
where the hell you are,

if you're well
and if you've made it out
alive.

Maybe I can't forget
that first time I saw you
or the last time either.

And don't tell me anything.

Don't tell me
you're not good enough
or that you don't do
and feel the same things
as I do.

Don't tell me
you don't have enough room
in you

for two people.

And lastly,
don't tell me
you don't believe in second chances.

Everyone deserves
at least one

and maybe that's
why we're still here.

LOVE BREAKS

Love breaks into madness
and sometimes
I can't control the things
you make me feel.

I'm crazy with you.
I'm crazy without you

and I don't care
what happens
inbetween.

THEY SAY

They say
they love you.
They say
they need you.

And they say
they will never leave.

Well, I say,
words aren't enough.

Show me you love me.
Show me you need me
and stay because you want to.

Because here,
words do not matter.

Because here,
actions outweigh everything.

And right now,
I need you to convince me
how it is easy to love,

not make it harder
than what
it already is.

DEMONS IN YOU

Your life
will make much more sense
when you learn
that the opinions of others
do not matter.

Know yourself.
Be kind to yourself.

The fight in you
belongs to you,

and how you defeat
your demons

is only something
that you can conquer
for yourself.

ALWAYS REMAINS

People change.

They are always transitioning
into something new,
something old.

So when I say
I appreciate you,
it only means
who you were,
who you are
and who you want to be.

So yeah,
people change,
times change,

but what will always remain
is the way
I admire you,

and to me,

that alone
might be the most beautiful
thing in the world.

SADNESS EATS ALL

One of the saddest things
in the world

is having too much
love in you

and

not having enough

words

to express
all that you feel.

NOT FOR PRIDE

There are many truths
but the one most people
seem to forget is,

that we all will be dead
longer than we are alive.

So why use
all this time fighting?

Why use
the time we are given,
trying to destroy
one another?

In a hundred years
everyone and everything
we know
will be gone,

evolved into something else.

So why not love
one another a little more?

Why not show the people
around you,
that you still care.

The world is far more beautiful
when we are together...

but the saddest truth is,
how most of us would
rather live and die alone.

And at what cause?
For pride?
For ego?
For power?

For all the things
we think
bring us closer together
but in reality
drift us all
further apart?

The world is far more beautiful
when we are together...

And I hope one day,
you will need me

because on *that day*
I will be there.

AND EVERY NIGHT

And every night
you feel more alone
than the night before.

And every night
the thoughts in your head
keep searching for answers.

And every night
you question the people
around you.

And every night
you wonder
and cannot help

but to wonder
if you should be doing
a little more.

And every night
you feel less like yourself
and more like a machine.

And every night
passes by you
and still,

you want more
but don't know
what to do
if you had more.

And every night
you're a different person,

so why not choose the one
you love most?

Why not be
who you *really* want to be?

Every night you have
the blessing to…

and every night you choose
to be someone else.

Ignoring your heart
can be deadly…

and being someone
you're not is suicide.

The human heart
cannot survive
without a little light.

THIS IS IT

No matter how bad
it hurts,

some people leave
to make you stronger,

while others times
they leave

to help you realize
how much
you've got
to love yourself.

IN FIVE YEARS

You want to be free
of pain
but you find the people
who hurt you
interesting.

You chase them,
want them,
and love them

as if they are meant
to save your life,

and maybe they are.

(Who knows.)

Maybe they are meant
for more than just
to cause a little pain.

Maybe they are meant
to teach you something,

so that five years
down the line
you could look back
and say,

"Thank you...
for making me
who I am."

HOW TO...

And once
you have given
someone
all of your love,
your tears
and your dreams...

it's kind of hard
to believe
in people again.

But none
will tell you this:

those who hurt you
only do it
because they're still searching
for something.

They want to love you
but they don't
understand

how to love themselves.

MY BEST ADVICE

You want to tell yourself
that you understand her,

that everything about her
is beautiful

but the truth is,
you don't know her.

You're not ready
for her sadness,
her faults and insecurities.

You're not ready
for the way she thinks
or feels.

You're not ready
for someone with
so much inside of her.

She knows
what she needs
because she tells me.

And sadly,
my young friend,

you're not ready
to love her
for who she is.

So let her go.
Let her be.

Stop filling her head
and heart
with mindless,
trivial things.

She has
her own feelings,
her own mind,
her own goddamn problems...

So please
stop feeding her heart
with all the bullshit

she clearly...
doesn't need.

A LITTLE SOUL

Now the people think
I'm a one percenter,
I'm
some kind of millionaire.

Well,
that's alright,
maybe I am
or maybe I am not.

*It doesn't matter
or make a difference.*

I'm still the same person,
with a bag
full of broken ideas
and a soul
aching to be held.

Money doesn't
change a person.

The person changes
once they have the money
and I'm still
the same person...

so what does that

have to say about that?

Besides
you're never *too rich*
in this earth,

at least not enough.

Money comes and goes
but your spirit is forever.

Kids,
I hope all of you
remember that

when I'm gone.

P. S.

Money can't buy you class
and I hope all of you

stay classy.

A GIRL

A girl from India
writes to me.

She asked why I don't ship
books to her country.

I tell her,

"Because USPS,
the postal service,
keeps losing
all of the international
shipments."

She immediately writes back
and mentions
how much of a shame it is.

How not having my books
is ruining her life.

Now I don't know her personally,
but it is not as bad
as she made it seem.

So some books
can't be mailed,
it is alright.

The world will carry on.

The thing is,
people need to see
their problem.

Analyze them
and realize
how small they truly are.

As for the world,
and its problems.

Where do I start?

What*is shameful* here is,
how the world
is in constant war.

How children have to die
and go to bed starving.

How people are truly left
with no one to talk to.

No one to go home to.
No home to go home to.

No drinking water
and no hope
other thanthe war

that rests before
their crying eyes.

It is a shame,
how we,
as a race
have evolved
and still,
do not have it in us
to save one another,
to help one another
and
to protect one another.

It is a shame,
a golden case full of it.

But above all,
the shame
of the shameful is

how USPS can't get
things right.

They can't keep
their shit together.

And it is a shame
how they fucking lose
nine out of every ten of my books
every damn time.

I guess that truth
has been left out.

Doesn't USPS understand
how education is the key
for change,
for salvation.

So please, USPS,
next time
treat my books with care.

For everyone knows
it is a book
that will save the world.

All the answers
to everyone's problems
can be found
between the pages

of the writers' sorrow.

UNTIL THEN, MAN

I'm still here,
waiting to make sense
of this torn love letter
in my pocket.

Waiting for the inspiration
to come find me.

Waiting for all the things
that connect,
so that I won't spill over
as I walk toward
your table.

The thing is,
I want to find you,

be with you

and I'll wait a life time
until then.

IT ONLY HURTS NOW

It only hurts
when it happens to you,
and it always
happens to you.

It happens so much
that you begin to believe
you're the only one.

But what most fail to see is
that everything
that happens to you
happens to us all.

Through ups
and downs

we all tend to feel
the same things
collectively.

So when some people say,
I've been there,

it's because they have
and you should listen to those
who have been broken,
beaten up

and have had enough things
happen to them.

Listen to these people,
get to know these people.

The more you understand them…
the more you will understand
yourself

and that is
the best thing
that can only happen

to you.

NEVER STOP

I know
I've said this
to you before
but I must repeat it
again and again.

I know you feel
as if you've been throughit all.

I know you feel
as if there's nothing out there
to complete you.

I know you feel alone,
empty
and at times,
you feel broken.

I know you feel
something,
but you don't know
how to explain it.

I know you feel
like no one understands you,
but trust me,
very few do.
I know your feet are tired

and your mind is restless.

I know you go through
the day
searching for more
because there is more.

*There's always
a little more.*

I feel you,
believe me I do.

Some people
never stop searching
for the right person
to hold.

FEEL FREE

She has me.

Like a fly
trapped on a web
and I'm not fighting it.

I'm all hers,
numb in love
and left undone

but I'm okay with that.

Sometimes,
with one look,

she makes me feel free.

She has me

and

I'm okay with that.

TOO MANY

There are too many
opportunities for you
to be happy
and yet,

you choose the people
who break you the most.

And because of that,

I am convinced,
that we,
no matter where we go,

we will always be infatuated
by the sting
that hurts the most.

That we,
as humans,

will always be attracted
to the things that destroy us.

That we want
what is best for us
but cling to the bad
that we forget

what it is
that makes us happy.

And we know this
and still
want the people
who may possibly be our doom.

We love them,
cry for them,
and we follow the horrors
of our hearts
as if salvation

is on the other side
of the door.

BEING YOU

Sooner or later
someone is going to grab you
by the hand
and remind you
how beautiful you are.

And it could be a lover,
a friend
or some random stranger.

Whoever it is,
I hope you believe it

and I hope
you take it all
in with good faith.

You have the whole
goddamn universe at the edge
of your fingers

and everyday
it brings you closer...

to being you.

IF ONLY I KNEW

The past is the hardest
to go back to

and

"if only I knew"

might be
the saddest thing
I have ever told myself

once you were gone.

If only I knew,
you didn't love me.

If only I knew,
I couldn't reach you.

If only I knew,
nothing could have saved me
from you.

If only I knew,
you wouldn't have stayed
long enough.

If only I knew,

we were going to
break each other
further apart.

And if only I knew,
how to walk away.

BACK HOME

Maybe you're made of more
than flesh and bone.

Maybe you're made of oceans,
moons and stars.

Maybe within you,

you have all the answers
to my questions,

all the miracles
to my prayers

and all the paths
I've ever needed

to find my way
back home

to you.

CONFESS

I must confess
that sometimes
I'm a horrible person.

That sometimes
I'm emotional
and say things to hurt you
and other people.

That sometimes
I find it in me
to bring you pain,
to bring hell fire
out of you.

Like sleepless nights
and self-chaos
the size of monuments.

So yes,
it is true,
my eyes are sad
just like you would say.

And yes,
they do not cry.

They cannot shed tears,

because I won't let them free.

I won't let them
do more
than what they are
supposed to.

I'm sorry
and I must confess,
that all these things are true,

which is why
I must admit
that I'm no good to you.

Perhaps,
that is why
you always feel this bitter emptiness
when you're around me.

Perhaps hope
is the only thing
that keeps you going.

You want me to change.
You want me to die,

to let go of the violent errors
that make me.

To reincarnate from the ashes

of what once was
and to find you
on the other side,
on the brighter side.

And yes,
I do want to take that step
but I am aware
of the beast within me,

that mad dog barking
within my heart,

that vicious wild animal
that *demands more* attention.

It's hard to let it go.

It's hard to watch it
live without me.

To watch it
find someone else
to depend on for its survival.

I'm sorry,
I just cannot.

I love the monster more,
which is what makes me
a horrible person.

That I cannot do something
for your well-being
because in all honesty,

I love myself more,
I trust myself more
and since the moment of birth
that's all I've really known...

that there's no right
or wrong here…

no good or bad,
just me,

alone and dragging my feet
across this forsaken earth.

I'm sorry,
and I must confess
that I will not change
unless I must.

I give myself to that belief,
that the machine that drives me.

I vow to it….

if I ever have to
I will destroy it

but ultimately,
if I must and ONLY
if it must

I will kill it

only because of me

and for me, alone.

I hope one day
you can understand that.

FIRES TO FEEL

And yes,
I've been called many things:

a storm,
a mistake,
a miracle
and a star...

but of all those things
being called yours
has set me free.

It has saved me
from all the hells
and all the fires

I was meant
to go through

and feel.

STARS (ENTRY)

I understood
why people got hurt,
and why they were always
okay with it,

that is,

if it only meant
they were going to feel
something.

Sometimes life felt long
and cruel,
while other times
it slipped right through
my fingers.

I understood this
and because of it,

I knew my heart was soft
and fragile.

I knew that at any given moment
my heart would break
the very instant
someone presented themselves
with a handful of stars.

If I wanted to love,
then it would arrive
unexpectedly and of course,

the moment it did,

I welcomed it.
And it didn't matter
if it was death knocking
at my front door.

True love was rare
and you were lucky enough
to have it arrive

at least once
every ten to fifteen years

or miss it.

You had to know it
when it presented itself

because sometimes,

that was your only change
to feel it

and if not

then it would completely

pass right over your head
and never come back
to you

at all.

You just had to know…

and never let opportunity
get lost.

It may be the only change
you get.

FALLING ON ROCKS

I like broken things
but not because they can be fixed
but because
broken things cannot be explained.

Because broken things
aren't really fragile.

Because broken things
don't need to try
to be beautiful...

they just are.

And like you,
broken things fall gently
and never asked to be held
and still,
they're held.

What I'm trying to say is,
I like you
because there are sides to you
that are hard
and unknown.

I think they're beautiful.
I want to hold you

when you feel most alone.

Be there for you.
Hold you, walk with you
and talk to you.

I want your universe
to rise and I want to howl

at the stars

the best way I can.

TODAY

Today the sky
reflects the sea.

Today your actions
reflect your thoughts.

Today your dreams
can be real.

Today the rain
fills the ocean.

And today
I feel the things
you feel.

Today we are together.
Today we don't fear tomorrow.

And everything else
is a moment waiting to happen,
and every second
of the day
could be spent
finding your way home.

Remember,
you must remember,

Today you are
the luckiest person
in the world.

Make it count.

Today everything
can still be yours.

TOO LATE AGAIN

"I'll never feel you again."

Those were the saddest words
I said to myself
over and over again.

But as time stretched
and I got older
I realized how in the end,
it's all the same.

People,
like wounds,
need their own space to heal,
and we do so alone
and at our own pace.

Time solves everything
and sometimes two people
aren't meant to stay…

but that's how it works.
That's how it ticks.

You give
and take
and if you're lucky enough
you'd leave with handful

of memories to last you
for years.

If only I had known
what I know now,

then perhaps,
the above wouldn't matter.

For too often
do people only listen
to themselves

when it is too late
and too often

it is *ALWAYS*
too late.

WANT TO NEED

People want to be loved
but they don't really
know what it feels like.

They don't really know
what it means.

And because of that,
most people want
what they don't understand.
And once they have it,

they realize
how some things aren't
what they seem.

What I'm trying to say is,
you should only love
because you want to

and not because
you think

you need to.

SAME SONGS

Everyone is listening
to the same songs,

watching the same
television shows,

reading the same books,
going to the same places,

and expecting
the same kind of love.

With all of that in place
you begin wonder
how anyone could ever be different,
when we are all forced
to believe and seek
the same things.

The same art.
The same love.
The same life.
The same dreams.

We want to make more money.
We want to eat right.
We want to have a big house.
We want to own more cars.

We want to have better businesses.
We want to have the perfect love.

We want. We want. We want.

We think we want.

We think. We think. We think.

It is all the same.
We think so much of what we want
that we forget
what it is we need.

We need to be ourselves.
We need to think for ourselves.
We need to do
what is right for ourselves
and no one else.

If you write a love letter
it should start with your name
and end with hope,

the one you have
for what you want
should be the same hope
for what you need.

You need to love yourself,
and that alone is something

they don't want you to have,
at least

not for yourself.

BY THE DOOR

The space between us
is beautiful.

You're there
and I'm here
and we could be together,

if only our egos
didn't stop us
by the door.

SOME WOMEN

I've learned how some women
would take it,

they would break everytime
someone told them
they loved them.

While at times,
other women couldn't stand it,

that is,

if you told them
you loved them,
and lied about it,

then that would be
the end for you.

The thing is,
some women are more
than just women.

Some women are dangerous,
they're warriors,

and they'll *eat
your fucking heart* out

the moment you tried
to ruin theirs.

I DO NOT KNOW

I've run out of things
to tell you.

I've run out of feelings,
ideas and heart.

I do not know
what the future holds.

I do not know
if we will be together.

All I know is,
now
and I don't want to stress
over the future
or live in the past…

because this is how it is.

This is how it should be.

Love now
and forget about the rest
right?

But this I tell you,
don't fall for me

goddamn it,
just don't.

I know you're infatuated
with my past,
and I know you want to be
in my future,

but don't.

This is not a good idea,
and I know how things like this
end, and they don't
end well.

Understand,
that I'm no good to you,
that I'm no good
to myself.

Hell, what am I saying.

The wolves have taken over.
My sanity is beyond
the grave
and the madness keeps pulling
at my hair.

The truth hurts,
as all things
people fall in love with

hurt.

And the thing is,
the steady reality
of it all is,

that I've been waiting
several years for someone like you
and now
I have nothing left to give.

I have run out of pieces to break.
I don't have enough for you.

So please,
just go,
there's nothing here left
to give.

SHE GOES

She goes
and sometimes far enough…

and I can't help
but to wonder,

how sometimes,
women like her

show you
how much they love you
with how far

they are willing
to walk away.

TYPEWRITER

I'm sorry
I don't love my typewriter
anymore.

I don't love
the machine.

The ink.
I don't love
the clunkyness,
the way the keys trap themselves
with each press.

I'm sorry
I don't love my typewriter
anymore.

We had a good run,
about seven years
of sorrow and happiness
and anger and love.

We shared too much together
and believed
we would be forever.

I'm sorry
I don't love my typewriter

anymore.

I've moved on,
I've outgrown it.

We no longer see
eye to eye.

I'm sorry
I don't love my typewriter
anymore.

There's so much more
than social media,
than posting excerpts
and killing myself over reviews.

I'm sorry
I don't love my typewriter
anymore.

I just don't.

I love the emotion,
the feeling,
the connection between my words
and other people.

I love what they hate
and I hate only one thing,
that I do not love

my typewriter
as I once did.

Damn.

I've moved on.

Damn.

I cannot finish this poem.
I can't stand it anymore.

Da…

WHAT THEY LOVE

The more people
I loved
the more I understood,

how sometimes
the greatest thing a person
could do is,

let the people say
what they feel

and let them become
what they love.

GETTING ALONG

I love seeing people
getting along.

I love believing
that maybe somewhere,
in some place,
two people
could look each other
in the eyes
without hatred eating away
at their hearts

and say,

"You're my friend."

The reward of peace
is beautiful,

and the reward
of true friendship
is even greater.

UNTITLED

I bought a Ruger
and I think
I did it
to exercise my right
to bear arms.

I don't know why
or when
or how
but I do know one thing.

One day,
the Ruger will come for me
it will weep for company

and when it does
I will be ready.

I will be calm…
and the world
will lose its lights

and I,

will be there.

AFTER OTHERS

Sometimes they want you
and sometimes they don't.

The same way
Somethings last
while others don't.

I guess,
what I'm trying to say is,
you don't have to chase people,

that is,

if they don't want you to.

If it's meant to be
then it will happen,
if not,
then you have a lot to realize,

and a lot to lose.

You should only chase people
who know
what running after others
is like.

THIS IS THE PART

This is the part
where you tell me
you love me
and leave.

This is the part
you give me a piece
of yourself
to take it away.

This is the part
you make me feel free
to trap me
in my own cage.

This is the part
I run toward you
so you could walk away.

I guess you could say,
some nights

I fall
into what's not really
there.

TO DO BOTH

You have to love yourself
before loving another person.

You have to have
enough courage
to save yourself,
fight for yourself
and find yourself,

before risking everything
at the price of true love.

And believe me,
the courage it takes
to love another person.

The courage it takes
to love yourself.

The courage it takes
to do both,

day in and day out.

Imagine that.

Now imagine losing everything
but still being lucky enough

to be alive.

The courage it takes
to face the world alone.

The courage it takes
to rise

and start all over
again.

NO ONE IS HERE

You have got to
let people grow
on their own

because sometimes

people get lost
the moment
they are found.

RAIN GIRL

Sad girl,
I see that your eyes
keep raining.

That your soul
keeps breaking,
and that your heart
keeps aching
for more.

Sad girl,
I see the flame of old love
on the edge of your eye.

The hurt
of past lives
and the lonely hour
of your memory.

Sad girl,
I know many things
bring you pain.

I know many things
falland many things
never learn
how to fly.

Sad girl,
do not lose hope…

please believe
that there are
a thousand beautiful things
waiting for you.

Sunshine comes
to *all* who feel rain.

YOU WIN, SOMETIMES

Understand,
that every second
is a miracle.

Understand,
how there will never be
anyone like you.

Understand,
that true love
does exist.

Understand,
that you will not
understand everything.

Understand,
that sometimes things
won't go your way.

Understand,
that losing someone
isn't always a bad thing.

Understand,
how growing up
never ends.

Understand,
that life isn't perfect
but enough to feel perfect.

Understand,
that you, at times,
will contradict yourself.

Understand,
that sometimes you'll win
but that someone
always
has to lose.

Understand all of these things
and I swear to you,

the love of the gods
will cover you
and it will never lead you stray.

Understand,
that all things divine
live and die

within you.

HEALS ALL

They say time heals
all wounds

and then

there's death,
and for you…

I'd die a million times
to relive

all the things
you once

made me feel.

STEP OUT

Step out of your flesh,
leave the calm of your ocean
and never return.

But do this
not for who you are
but for
who you will become.

Do this
not for the things
you love
but for the things
that hurt.

Do this
not for what brings you peace
but for what disrupts
the heart.

Do this
not for what you know
but for the unknowns
that await you
on the other side.

Do this
not for people,

but for memories,
for glory.

Do this
not to show the world
that you are worthy
of being remembered
but to show yourself
you can do anything
you put your mind to.

Step out of yourself
to find yourself.

Do it.

Do it now.

Before the world
tells you who you are...

and before...

you lose track
of whom you want to
become.

THE BEST THINGS

This life,
for all that it is,
it is all
about perception.

It is all
about what you make it
and how you make it,

for what it is.

By that I mean,
how sometimes,
the best things in life
don't necessarily mean

they are the best things
for everyone.

Sometimes the worse things
can be the best things

and sometimes

the best things
can mean nothing
at all.

SEVEN BILLION

There are seven billion faces,
and at a certain point
of their lives
they will each look
for something.

Most search
for the same thing:

love, sex, money,
fame, etc.

In this great journey,
in this search,
most will find hatred,
racism, and discrimination.

They will run
into a burning wall.

And it doesn't matter
how long they've been searching.

Somewhere down the line
these terrible things
will find them,
to stop them from what it is
they are seeking,

from what it is *you're seeking.*

And these people
will feel pain.
They will tear
and sweat
and walk in fear.

They will struggle
and continue to endure
during this great search.

Eventually,
these special people
do find
what they are looking for.

And they will seem
as if
they have fulfilled their lives.

They will talk about their glory
and drift into the night
in holy laughter.

And as the sun rises
a new day is given,
new breath is given
and revelations are born.

These people,

these seven billion faces
do what they think
is good for them,

and waste their lives
chasing it.

To only discover
that when they find
what they are seeking,

Their lives have walked
right by them
and they are left distorted,
lost

in their own void.

Find your own truth
and no one else's.

AMEN.

KEEP GOING

I've always had
this feeling
that you were no good
for me.

I've always felt it
in the middle of my bones
but nonetheless,

I want to thank you
for giving my heart
a chance to move on.

For sometimes
you're forced into the
darkest of places
and sometimes

those same people
give you no choice
but to keep going.

BECOMING ICE

They say,
thatI have become cold,
hard and unbreakable.

I say,
that I have become
all of those things
because I have finally learned
how to look out
for myself,
care for myself.

I love me
before I love you.

Now I know
that sounds selfish
but it is true.

So yes,
maybe I am cold,
hard and unbreakable.

Yes, fucker,
I am the goddamn snow blizzard
you wish
you could outrun,

and I'm coming
like a bullet.

So whether you move
or stand,
or hold your breath
or let go…

to choose
to live or die

is completely
up to you.

BORN INTO...

When a baby is born.

When a person saves
someone from death.

When a forest is born
from one tree.

When people find themselves
after years of searching.

When two people feel love
for the very first time.

When someone isn't near
but they seem
closer than ever.

When it rains.
When you kiss.

Every time
you take breath.

When you feel alone
and someone thinks of you.

When a revelation answers

your prayers.

When you tell someone
you miss them
and they feel the same way.

Miracles come
in all shapes and sizes.

All you have to do
is pay attention.

A miracle
is always

waiting to happen.

RELIGION

I know nothing
of religion
and yet,
I speak of miracles
as if
I've met god.

I know nothing
of prayer
and yet,
I've been given a mind
and a pen
and the power
to love.

I know nothing
of people
and yet,
they all feel connected
to the words
that appear
across my heart.

I know nothing
of nothing
but I feel
what I have to feel
to make others

feel something.

I know nothing else
but this.

Maybe god does have a way
of communicating with others.

And maybe
I am nothing more
but his pen,
his words,
thoughts and feelings.

You're not alone.

You never have been
and you never will be.

There is a god
always looking out for you

and always willing
to listen
to what hurts you.

NO MATTER

No matter who you know,
who you love
or what you do.

Do not cage
your heart
for other people.

You must understand
that your soul
is a star

and it needs
its own space
to breathe.

GIVEN TIME

You've got to keep
the kind of people
that make you feel
as if

you could achieve
the impossible…

at any given time.

NOW NOW NOW

Now that we have lost,
felt pain and cried.

Now that we have tasted
the violent, bitter flavor
of death.

Now that we have
seen too much
and lived even more.

Now that we have
gone far enough,
to stand over the edge
of change.

Now that we have
forgotten what worries us,
moves us and makes us
who we are.

Now,
when there is nothing left
to do…

let us all
remember one thing…
to love, heal and grow.

Let us all
arrive in a place
where hands seek
other hands

and eyes
seek other eyes
and hearts
seek other hearts,

to remind themselves
of why we should love

others

the same.

WHAT MATTERS MOST

Sometimes,
the only things that matter
are lost
and very few times

do those same things
return to their
rightful owners.

That's why
when you have something special,
something worth it,
you care for it.

You don't let the things
that make your heart skip
slip away.

GET TOO CLOSE

You've got to
let people get close.

You've got to
let them be there for you
no matter how isolated
you feel.

You've got to
let them help you
and support
what you stand for.

Let them in,
for some people are genuinely
good people.

That some doors
are meant to be left open
and not broken down
by the seeker.

Listen to them,
get to know them
and understand
how you receive
what you put out.
Understand that solitude

can be beautiful
but it can also be
destructive.

Understand
that yes,
some people can empty you
but also,
some people
can save you
from the hollowness
of your soul.

Understand
that not everyone
is out to ruin you,

that some people
really want to see
your magnificent glory
in all colors.

Let these people in,
they're everywhere.

Let them eat with you,
sleep, breathe and live
by you side.

Let them cry,
pray and love.

Let them in.

let them come through
the door without knocking
and without

you asking
who's there.

God bless.

GOES ON

You need to believe
in the power of friendship
and the significance
of strength in numbers.

And remember,
it's your role
to love as many people
as you can

and never forget
how people

can either break
or get stronger
as time goes on.

SHE CRIED

And she cried
as if falling apart
was a beautiful thing
to do.

But in the end,
I didn't want to see her broken,

I didn't want to see her sad
and full of tears.

I wanted her to ride her life
off the rails,

to fall off the edge
of the moon
and land
head first into the sun.

If it only led her
to crash

toward the inspiration
she was meant
to have.

DISCOVER TIME

Together we fall
beneath the black sky
and exchange
all the things we feel.

We say
we love each other
more than anything
else

and for some reason,

I cannot help
but to feel,

like I'm just
discovering something
that's been around

for a very
long time.

RULES AND LAWS

People need rules,
routines,
something to tell them
what to do.

I mean,
take a look at our lives.

We wake up,
go to work,
make someone else money
and then
we go home
to wake up
and do the same thing
the next day.

And some will say
that this is life,

that this is
the way it's supposed to be
but I think they're wrong.

I think there's more
to live for.

For example,

you take a wild bird
and cage it
and it might die

and then
you take a caged bird
and free it
and it will soar beyond
what the eyes could see,

and it's the same way
with people.

You give them the freedom
they deserve
and they will be inspired
to do even more.

They will break the rules
and make the world
a better place.

I know it
and so should you.

WE COULD HAVE

Sometimes I think about you,
and I wonder
why we never gave
each other a chance.

Maybe it was me
or you
or the distance between us
but I know
if you were here
things would be different.

Maybe you and I
could have been something.

Maybe we could have
been happy

and we could have changed
each other's lives.

I THINK OF YOU

Sometimes
I think about you,
and I wonder

why we never gave
each other a chance.

Maybe it was me
or you
or the distance between us
but I know
if you were here
things would be different.

Maybe you and I
could have been something.

Maybe we could have been happy
and we could have changed

each other's lives.

CPSIA information can be obtained
at www.ICGtesting.com
Printed in the USA
LVOW03s1237120418
573066LV00001B/1/P